This book belongs to:

....

Contents

Peppa Pig

Fun at the Fair

Today, Peppa and her family are at the funfair.
"Snort! Slidey, slidey!" giggles George.
"George wants to go on the
helter-skelter," says Daddy Pig.
Daddy Pig and George head off to
the helter-skelter.

"Roll up! Roll up!" cries Miss Rabbit.
"Hook a duck and win a giant teddy!"
"I'll try to win one for you, Peppa," says
Mummy Pig. "But I don't think it's that easy!"
"It's impossible!" laughs Miss Rabbit.
"We'll see about that!" cries Mummy Pig.

Sploosh! Mummy Pig has hooked a duck!

"Hooray!" cheers Peppa.

"That's amazing!" cries Miss Rabbit.

"Here's your giant teddy!"

"Wouldn't you like a little teddy instead, Peppa?"

"No way!" giggles Peppa, happily.

George and Daddy Pig are at the helter-skelter.
"Hmm, it's a bit high, George. Are you sure you
want to have a go?" asks Daddy Pig.
George giggles and runs up the stairs to the top.
It's a bit too high and George starts to cry.
"Don't worry, George. I'll come up with you,"
says Daddy Pig.

"Hee, hee! Weeeeeeee!" cries George,
sliding all the way down the helter-skelter.
Now, George is having too much fun to be scared.
"It is a bit high," says Daddy Pig nervously.
Daddy Pig is more scared than George.
Oops! Daddy Pig slips down the slide!

Wooahhh!

Peppa and Mummy Pig are at the
'Hit the Target' stall.

"You can do that easily, Mummy," says Peppa.

"Ho, ho! You won't win!" laughs Mr Labrador.

"Women are useless at this!"

"What did you say?" says Mummy Pig crossly.

She picks up the bow and arrow and aims . . .

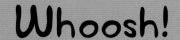

Whoosh!

The arrow hits the target
right in the middle.

Mummy Pig wins again!

"Unbelievable," cries Mr Labrador. "Here's your teddy!"

"Hooray!" cheers Peppa.

Now she has two giant teddies.

Daddy Pig and George are
riding on the big wheel. George loves it,
but Daddy Pig is a little bit scared.
"This really is high!" says Daddy Pig, as the
big wheel goes round and round.
"Hee, hee! Snort!" giggles George.

Daddy Pig and George find Peppa and Mummy Pig.
"Hit this button with a hammer," says
Mr Bull. "If the bell rings, you win a prize!"
"I'll have a go," says Daddy Pig. "Stand back!"
"I think you're a bit wobbly from the big wheel!"
says Mummy Pig.

"Ho, ho!" laughs Mr Bull.
"Daddy Pig is looking a bit shaky!"

"What?" says Mummy Pig, crossly.
"Give . . . me . . . that . . . hammer!"
Whack! Mummy Pig hits the button
as hard as she can.
The bell rings loudly. Ding! Ding! Ding!

Everyone is very impressed. Mummy Pig wins
all the giant teddies at the fair!

"Hooray!" cheers Peppa and she gives all of
her friends one giant teddy bear each.
"Hooray!" everyone cheers. "We love funfairs!"

George's First Day at Playgroup

Today is George's first day at playgroup.
"Isn't George too small for playgroup?" asks Peppa.
"You can look after him," says Daddy Pig.
Peppa isn't sure she wants George at
her playgroup, but she likes the idea of
looking after him.

"Are you sure George is big enough?"

Peppa asks when they arrive.

"Yes, he'll be fine," replies Daddy Pig.

"OK. He can come," says Peppa.

She holds onto George's hand.

"Grunt! Grunt!" snorts George, jumping

up and down.

Here is Madame Gazelle, Peppa's playgroup teacher. She looks after Peppa and her friends. Madame Gazelle tells the children that George is coming to play. The children are all very excited about meeting Peppa's little brother.

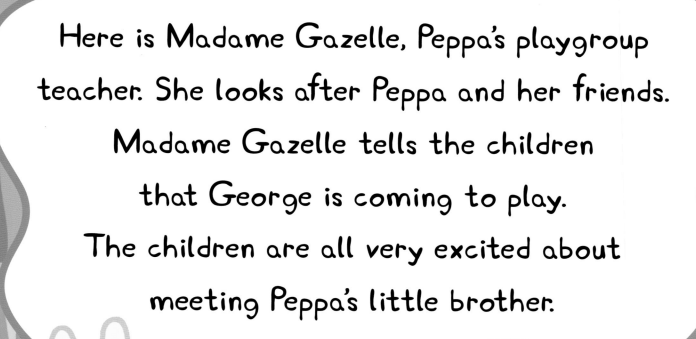

George shakes his toy, Mr Dinosaur, at Madame Gazelle, "Grrr! Dine-saw!" "Aah! Really scary!" laughs Madame Gazelle. Peppa is proud of George making everyone laugh. "George is my little brother. He's brilliant," she says.

"Watch me, George," snorts Peppa.
"First, you paint a big circle."

Peppa carefully dips her brush into a pot of
pink paint and draws a big pink circle
right in the middle of her paper.

George draws a big green circle.

"No, George. That's the wrong colour,"

snorts Peppa. "Watch me."

Peppa makes yellow petal shapes.

George paints a green zigzag.

"George! That's the wrong shape," says Peppa.

Peppa admires her flower painting.
"Perfect," she says, happily.
George is still painting. Instead of a stalk
and leaves he has painted another circle
with five lines sticking out from it.
"You are doing it all wrong!" says Peppa.

"I've painted a flower," says Peppa.

"Very good, Peppa," smiles Madame Gazelle.

"And look, George has painted a dinosaur."

Madame Gazelle sticks Peppa and George's

pictures on the wall.

Now it is time to go home.
"What will you paint next time,
George?" asks Madame Gazelle.
"Dine-saw! Grrr!" giggles George.
"Hee, hee, hee!" everyone laughs.

Peppa Pig™

Peppa Goes Camping

Today, Peppa and George
are very excited.
They are going on holiday!
Daddy Pig has a surprise.
Honk, honk!

"It's a camper van," grunts Daddy Pig.
"Wow!" gasp Peppa and George.

"We're going on holiday!" sings Peppa.

"We're going on holiday, in our camper van! Snort!"

"Hmmm," says Daddy Pig, looking at the map.

"Daddy Pig!" cries Mummy Pig. "Are we lost?"

"Well, er," begins Daddy Pig, "yes!"

Granddad Dog and Danny Dog arrive.
"Hello," calls out Peppa. "We're lost!"

"Lost?" asks Granddad Dog, confused.
"Is your satnav broken?"
Peppa, George, Mummy and Daddy Pig
don't know what satnav is.

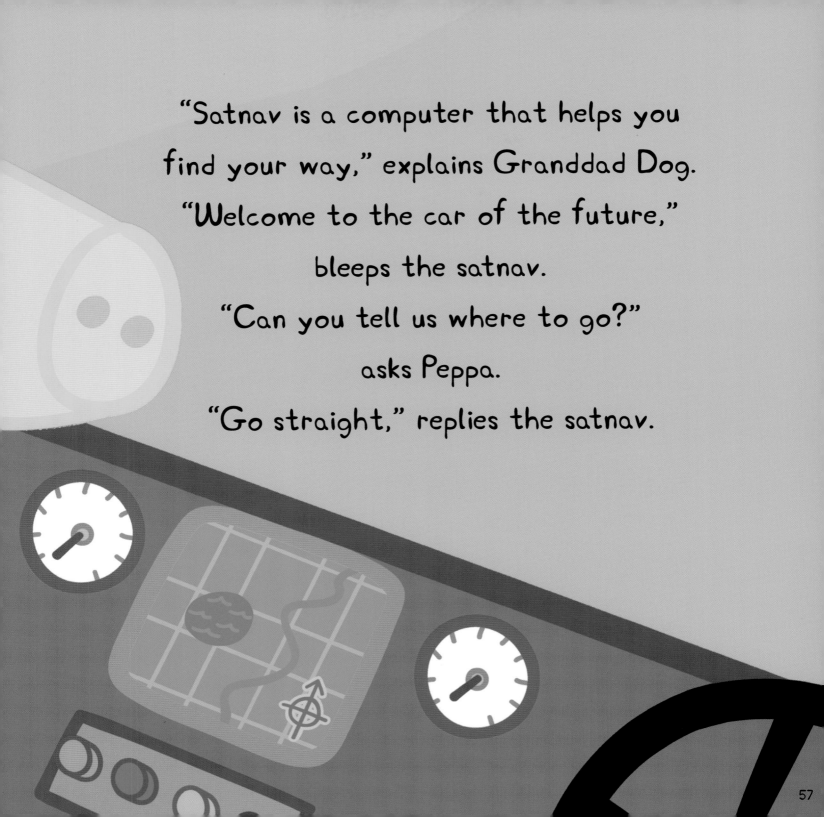

"Satnav is a computer that helps you find your way," explains Granddad Dog. "Welcome to the car of the future," bleeps the satnav.

"Can you tell us where to go?" asks Peppa.

"Go straight," replies the satnav.

Daddy Pig thanks Granddad Dog
and the family continue on their way.
"We're going on holiday," sings Peppa.
"We're going on holiday, in our camper van!"
Suddenly, the camper van is low on oil.
But Daddy Pig can't find the engine!

"Are we nearly there yet?" asks Peppa, sighing.

"Just up the next hill," says the satnav.

"You have reached your destination," says the satnav when they get to the top of a steep hill.

"Hooray!" everyone cheers.

"Ta-da! A lovely big bed appears in the room.

"And you two will sleep upstairs like you always do," says Mummy Pig.

"Watch this," says Daddy Pig, pressing another button.

Whirrr! Click . . .

Snore!

Snore!

Snore!

Snore!

Peppa Pig™

Peppa Plays Football

It's a sunny day and Peppa Pig and
Suzy Sheep are playing tennis.
"To you, Suzy!" cheers Peppa, hitting
the ball. Now it's Suzy's turn.
"To you, Peppa!" she cries, hitting the ball
straight over Peppa's head. Oh dear!

Peppa and Suzy are having lots of fun,
but they keep missing the ball.
"Ball boy!" they shout together.
"Huff, puff!" George is not having fun.
He keeps running to get the ball and
he is very tired!

"We can play girls against boys," says Peppa.
"Each team needs a goalkeeper," says Danny Dog.
"Me, me!" shouts Pedro Pony.
"Me, me!" cries Rebecca Rabbit.

83

Pedro Pony and Rebecca Rabbit
decide to be the goalkeepers.
"The boys' team will start!" says Danny Dog.
Richard Rabbit gets the ball and runs
very fast, right by Peppa Pig,
Suzy Sheep and Candy Cat
and straight up to the . . .

"That goal is not allowed," says Pedro.

"Yes, it is," says Peppa.

"No, it isn't!" barks Danny.

"What a lot of noise," snorts Daddy Pig.

"I'll be the referee.

The next team to

get a goal will win

the game."

Richard Rabbit and George run off with the
football, while everyone is still talking.
"Where's the ball?" asks Peppa.
But it's too late! Richard Rabbit kicks the
ball straight into the goal, past Pedro Pony.
"Hooray! The boys win!" cries Danny.

93

"Football is a silly game," sighs Peppa, disappointed. "Just a moment," says Daddy Pig. "The boys scored in their own goal, that means the girls win!"

"Really?" gasp all the girls. "Hooray!"

"Football is a great game!" cheers Peppa.

"Ha, ha, ha!" everyone laughs.

School Bus Trip

Peppa and her friends are going on a school bus trip.

Woof!

98

"Let's check you are all here,"
says Madame Gazelle.
"Here!" cries Peppa.

Baaa! Grunt! Snort!

"Today," begins Madame Gazelle, "we are going on a trip to the mountains!"

"Hooray!"
cheer all the children.

Peppa and Suzy are
already a little hungry.
"Please can we eat our lunch now?"
they ask Madame Gazelle.

102

"Why not eat your apples and save the rest for the picnic?" she replies. Crunch! Crunch!

The bus has arrived at the foot of the mountain. The road is very steep! "Come on, bus! You can make it!" everyone cheers.

Peppa and her friends have finally made it
to the top of the mountain.
"Look at the view!" gasps Madame Gazelle.
All the children look out over the valley.

"Wow!" sighs Peppa, loudly.
"Wow! Wow! Wow!" Peppa hears
in the distance.
"What was that?" she asks quietly.
"It's your echo, Peppa!"
replies Madame Gazelle.

"An echo is the sound you hear when you speak loudly in the mountains," explains Madame Gazelle.
Grunt! Woof! Baaa! Snort!

Now it's time for a picnic lunch.
Peppa loves picnics. Everyone loves
picnics! Munch! Slurp! Munch!
Yum! Yum!

"Where are the ducks?" asks Peppa, taking a bite of her sandwich. "They always turn up when we have picnics."

Quack! Quack! Quack!
Here come the ducks.

"Hello! Would you like some bread?"
Peppa asks them. The ducks are very lucky today.
There is plenty of bread!

117

The bus has arrived.
It's time to go home.

"Let's all sing a song!" suggests
Madame Gazelle. Hooray!
Everyone has had a great day!

Peppa Goes Swimming

It's a lovely sunny day and Peppa and her family are at the swimming pool.

"Peppa! George! Let Daddy put on your armbands," snorts Mummy Pig.

123

Splash! Mummy Pig convinces George to jump into the water and he loves it!

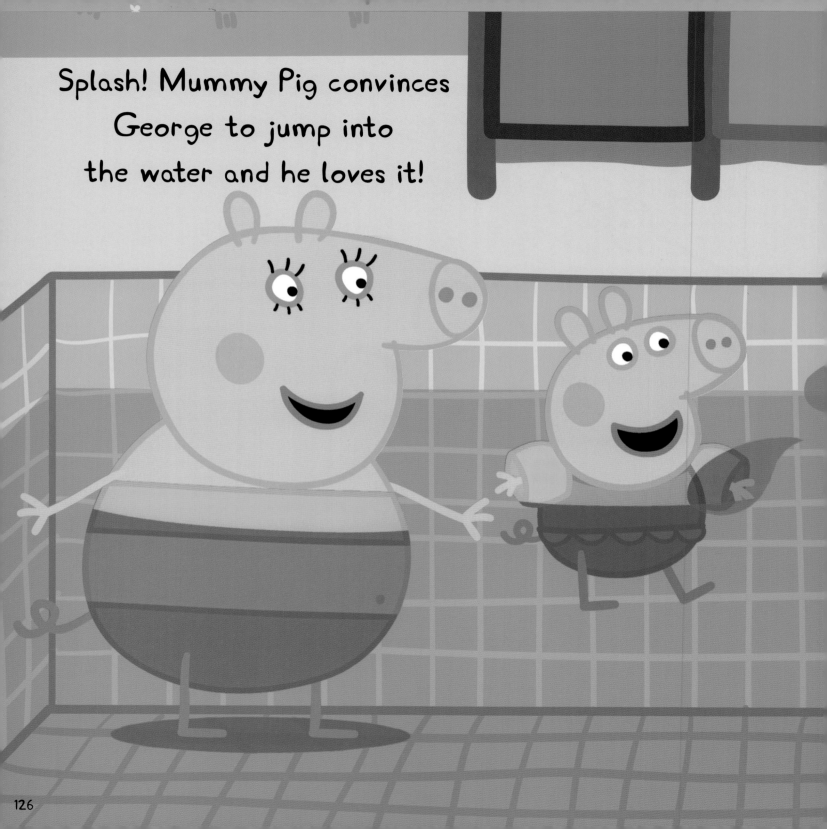

126

"Grunt! Hee! Hee! Snort!"
shouts George, happily.
"Ho! Ho! Well done, George!"
snorts Daddy Pig.

"Richard, hold on to this float
and you can practise kicking your legs,"
says Mummy Rabbit.

"George, would you like to try
kicking your legs?" asks Mummy Pig.
"Hee! Hee! Float! Snort!" giggles George.

"Ho! Ho! Very good," laughs Daddy Pig, "but please try not to splash." "Grunt! Big children don't splash," adds Peppa.

"Big children are very good at swimming," snorts Peppa. "When George and Richard are older, they'll be able to swim like us, won't they, Rebecca?"

"Yes!" says Rebecca, as she
watches the boys kicking.

Peppa and Rebecca race each other up and down
the pool with their armbands on.

They are having lots of fun swimming
and splashing in the water.

Oops! Richard has dropped his toy
watering can into the pool.
"Mummy! Wah!" cries Richard.
"Sorry, Richard, I can't reach.
It's too far down," says Mummy Rabbit.
Luckily, Daddy Pig is an excellent swimmer.
He takes off his glasses and dives down to get it.

"Ho! Ho! There you go!"
snorts Daddy Pig.
"Squeak, squeak!" says Richard.

"Well done, Daddy!"
smiles Mummy Pig.

Oh dear! Now Richard is soaking Daddy Pig
with the watering can. What a naughty Rabbit!
"Hee! Hee! Hee!" George thinks it's hilarious.
Everyone has had a wonderful day at the pool!